Hi There
My Name Is Edward,
Can You
Open This Book
and Find Me?

Carole J. (Fleischauer) Noelle

" Carole Noelle "

PAGE PUBLISHING, INC.
New York, NY

First originally published by Page Publishing, Inc. 2016

ISBN 978-1-68213-803-8 (pbk)
ISBN 978-1-68213-804-5 (digital)

Printed in the United States of America

DEDICATION

To ALL children who love animals and can or cannot have their own pet. Edward will be "your" pet while you look for and find him.

Thank you for loving Edward!

I want to introduce you to
Taco and Phoenix.
They love to chase me, but
they are very gentle
And never hurt me.

But sometimes, I need to get
away. See if you can
Find all of my hiding places. Good luck!

When I hide here, Taco and Phoenix, my dog brother and sister can't find me. Can you?

4

My mom tells me not to go in here, but it's soft and cozy. Do you know where I am?

Do you know where I am now? Taco and Phoenix are looking all over. Shhhhh. Don't tell them.

My mom filled this big box
with little boxes, but I'm still
trying to hide in here.
If I'd be quiet, maybe Taco and
Phoenix won't find me. Will you?

You have been doing so great, and you are so smart. Do you know where I am this time?

12

I hope my mom doesn't close the door to the laundry closet. 'Cause I'm in here!

14

You found all my hiding
places. And now,

THIS IS THE END.

16

ABOUT THE AUTHOR

Carole Noelle lives in Moose Lake, Mn. After raising 5 children and working in healthcare for 30 years, she retired. She still works to take care of disabled children.

She adopted Edward and Phoenix and got Taco as a puppy for companionship.

Edward loves finding hiding places and is a very fun pet.

Hopefully everyone will enjoy Edwards' story.

CPSIA information can be obtained at www.ICGtesting.com
Printed in the USA
BVOW10s2124290216

438543BV00003B/3/P